PUFFIN BOOKS

Editor: Kaye Webb

BEL THE GIANT

AND OTHER STORIES

There was once a giant who got all the food he wanted by bullying the farmers, and a family of little rabbits who couldn't find their front door in the snow, and a magic walking stick, and a little boy who was really a seal, and a tangerine cat who learned to play the fiddle . . .

But we mustn't give away any more secrets about these stories except that they are by Helen Clare, author of *Five Dolls in a House*, who has the marvellous story-telling gift for making something fresh and interesting out of even the simplest tale. As one reviewer has said: 'She writes with grace and clarity, and touches on things that matter.'

HELEN CLARE

BEL THE GIANT

AND OTHER STORIES

Illustrated by Peggy Fortnum

PENGUIN BOOKS

Penguin Books Ltd, Harmondsworth, Middlesex, England
Penguin Books Australia Ltd, Ringwood, Victoria, Australia

—

First published by The Bodley Head 1956
Published in Puffin Books 1971

—

Made and printed in Great Britain by
Cox & Wyman Ltd, London, Reading and Fakenham
Set in Monotype Baskerville

For Jill and Paul

Contents

Bel the Giant

ONCE upon a time there was a giant lived in Leicestershire, and his name was Bel. Now the worst thing about the giant Bel was the way he bragged and boasted. When an ordinary person brags and boasts, he can be put in his place. But when a giant swaggers over the hedges, boasting he can jump six haystacks in a row, there is nothing to be done. Of course he can.

'Of course,' said the people of Leicestershire, 'if we had legs as long as an elm branch, and toenails the size of a Melton pie, so could we.'

But they hadn't, so they couldn't. And the giant

Bel went on boasting and annoying the people of Leicestershire. As well as this he was a great nuisance other ways. Imagine how much a giant of his size eats. The giant Bel would eat at one meal a bullock and a pig and six cheeses and a dozen chickens. As for fruit, he would pick a well-laden apple bough, and strip off the apples with his teeth, as ordinary people do a bunch of red-currants. But as he was lazy and could not be bothered to tend his own sheep, pasture his own cows, or make his own cheeses, he must needs go round all the farms in Leicestershire demanding food. Sometimes, when the farmers heard a noise like thunder and a roaring as if the wind were getting up, they would run to their fields and drive in their animals, for they knew it was the giant Bel. But it was seldom any use. The giant Bel took such giant strides that he was there before they could turn a cow. And if they refused to give him his dinner, he simply came along spitefully and kicked over their barns with the toe of his boot, *poof!* Like that.

But when Bel said *Poof!* the straw blew about the farm-yard, and the chickens were puffed into the corner of a distant field, and the dairy door blew open, and the fires smoked, and the farmer's wife lost her breath and sat panting for an hour. So nobody liked Bel saying *Poof*.

And if they still would not give him his dinner he would come along at night and rip off the farmhouse thatch between his thumb and his great first finger which had a ring on it the size of a turnip. And there would be the farmer and his wife and his sons and his daughters in their beds, with no roof. And Bel would choose a rainy night, and he would go away laughing as the farmer was rained on in his bed. Therefore it is not to be wondered at that the people of Leicestershire did not care for Bel the giant.

There was a farmer called Farmer Hook, who had just spent a month or two fixing on the thatch that Bel the giant had pulled off. He was very tired of Bel the giant. When he heard the distant thunder of his feet and the puff of his breath, he decided that he would stand up to him, once and for all. It was no good fighting, for of course he wouldn't win. It was no good arguing if the giant were hungry. He thought out a clever plan and waited.

Now this Farmer Hook had a very fine bay

mare, called Jennet. She was the best mare, he always said, who ever rode to hounds. Bel the giant meanwhile had an enormous sorrel charger to fit himself, though there's no knowing where he got him. No such giant horse was ever bred in the shires. The giant was very proud of his sorrel charger, as Farmer Hook knew.

In a few minutes there was a cloud against the sky, and in strode the giant Bel to Farmer's field.

'Hey, Farmer, I'll thank you for a young and juicy bullock. Or would you rather I ate you?'

'Wait a bit, wait a bit. There's time for that. Have you ever seen my fine mare Jennet?'

And Farmer got him talking about Jennet.

'Poof!' said Bel (and all the straw in the stable blew up and down again). 'Fine mare, indeed! Did you ever see my sorrel charger? There's a horse for you if you like.'

'I say Jennet's a fine mare,' said Farmer. 'Why, she will carry me to Leicester in the half of an hour.'

'The half of an hour!' bellowed the giant, and laughed enough to scare the sheep out of their fleeces. 'I could get to Leicester on my charger in

three leaps! Three leaps from this very spot, or I'm not Bel the giant.'

'That I don't believe,' said Farmer. 'It's nearly seven miles to Leicester.'

'Poof! Then I'll make you believe it,' said Bel, and over went one of Farmer's haystacks and bowled half way across a field. 'What will you give me if I do?'

'If you reach Leicester in three leaps,' said Farmer, scratching his head, 'I'll give you all my sheep and all my cattle and I'll go and seek my fortune somewhere else,' he said.

So the day came for the giant to try, and all along the countryside to Leicester the people gathered to see. There was Bel, in his great coat, and his great boots like tree trunks and his great spurs like drawn swords, and his great whip which sounded like fifty guns when he cracked it.

He puffed himself out and he boasted, until there was such a wind the people had to hold their hats on.

At a place near Farmer's house, he mounted his great sorrel charger. And that place is called *Mountsorrel* to this day.

He gathered himself up, he called to his steed,

14

and away he went, up in the air, a great long leap, and the people of Mountsorrel said, 'O–o–oh!' as he disappeared. In one leap he reached a place a half of the way to Leicester. And that place has been called *Wanlip* ever since. All the people at Wanlip gazed to see the giant land.

Then Bel drew himself up, and he roared at his charger, and he leapt again, and all the people said, 'There he goes!' as he soared through the air.

But then there was a terrible bursting and cracking noise, a noise like whips of leather, a roaring noise like a tree falling down. It was Bel's harness, Bel's horse, and Bel's bones themselves, bursting with the great long leap.

With a sigh like a storm at sea he came down *galumph* at a place two thirds of the way to Leicester. And that place has been called *Birstall*, ever since.

Bel groaned and thought of the farmer's sheep and cattle. He urged on his dying charger with the great spurs, he gave an echoing shout, and away he went again with his harness flying in all directions. (Some of the children ran to pick up the pieces.)

But Bel had boasted too much. It was too long a leap for him, too great an effort for his great sorrel charger. He came down groaning like a winter wind at a place a mile and a half from Leicester. And there they rolled over dead, the boastful giant Bel and his sorrel charger. They were buried in one great grave where they landed, and that place has been called *Belgrave* from that day to this.

As for the people round Leicester, they rejoiced greatly to know the greedy and boastful giant was dead, and their sheep and cattle safe. Especially Farmer Hook and his beautiful bay mare Jennet. He and his wife and his children danced round Jennet singing a rhyme, and this is the rhyme they sang:

> 'Mountsorrel he mounted at
> Rothely he rode by,
> Wanlip he leaped o'er,
> At Birstall he burst his gall,
> At Belgrave he was buried at.'

You may still hear it sometimes, in Leicester-shire.

The Selkie Boy

ONCE upon a time and many years ago, there was a little boy called Willie who lived in the northernmost tip of the Orkney Isles, which lie washed by the grey sea off the northernmost point of Scotland. Here Willie lived, in a grey stone house, with the kail yard around it and the cows' byres near it and the sheep above it, and always in sound of the sea. Now the father in the house was a farmer, and a fisher, but he was not Willie's father. And the mother in the house was a good wife and careful, but she was not Willie's mother. And the six other bairns of the steading were bonny enough and happy enough, but they were not Willie's sisters and brothers. And although they sometimes played with Willie, they just as often left him out, until he used to feel forlorn. And although their father and mother were kind enough to Willie, they did not really understand him. For Willie was different from the others. He was a dreamy bairn, and happiest when he lay sleepy in the sun all by himself. When the

children left him out of their games, he would go
to the shore and pick up whelks and limpets along

the ebb, and then lie
out and sun himself for
all the world like a little
selkie.

Now the selkies were
the seals that swam and
basked in numbers,
round the rocks and in
the skerries, near the
shores of Ronaldsay.

Sometimes when his
sisters and brothers were
playing handy-croopen,
or barley, or king makes
captives, they would
call to Willie to come.

'Come on, Willie,
sleepy Willie!'

But he would shake

his head and watch them as they said their
rhymes.

'Etem, petem, penny pie,
Popalorum, jinkum jie,
Esas, esink,
Peas, pottage,
Small drink,
Thou art once out,'

they chanted, round and round, sing-song fashion,
to find who should be king. And often they teased
Willie and were not over kind. Now this was
because they were a little frightened of him, he
was so different.

'Where did you come from, Willie?' they
teased.

'The trows brought you and the trows will take
you again!'

'Hush,' said their mother. 'You mustn't tease
wee Willie and you mustn't talk about the grey
folk of the crags.'

For the fact was, nobody quite knew where wee

Willie had come from. Fishermen had found him, a little fellow with yellow hair, playing on the shore one day when the tide was low. And when they asked him where his mother was, he could not tell them. He was too little to speak and he seemed lost, though he was happy enough playing with the stones.

'We cannot leave the bairn in the foam,' said the men, and they brought him to the good wife at the farm. And there he was ever since, growing up the prettiest boy in the island. Some people said he was a changeling, and left by the trows, the good folk, and that he would go as quietly as he came. Some said his mother and father must have been drowned, and Willie happened to reach shore. But there was no wreck the day Willie came, and the sea was as bright and as sparkling as a fairy tune, and smooth as the milk in the pail. So it was very strange. And some said he was a selkie child, who had lost his skin

and could not go back to
his green home.

'For selkie folk, they
cannot go back if they
have no skin,' said the
wise women.

Certainly Willie loved
the sea and loved the
selkies, and would often
go to the shore to watch
them. He loved every-
thing about the sea. Long

and long he would wait, hoping to see a tangle,
the little green horse that comes dressed in sea
weed up the waves.

Many a day in summer, when Willie was lying
basking in the sun, he would fall asleep to the tune
of the gentle waves beating on the sand, and dream
he was riding a green horse out to the deep water.
When he awoke he would look out to the deep rocks,
and there were the selkies, twisting and turning
with the sun sliding off them. Then Willie would run
on his bare feet down to the surf edge and stand
in the powdery brown foam and watch them with
his eyes eager and as green themselves as the sea.

'If I could swim like the selkies!' he would sigh.

To tell the truth, Willie could swim and very strongly. When the weather was not too cool, he and the others would go swimming in the clear, cold burns, or down on the shore where there were no rocks. Willie could swim farther and faster than any, even when he was only a tiny bairn.

'Where did you learn your swimming, wee Willie?' called the rest, when they saw him slicing the water with his strong arms.

'It's a secret,' said Willie.

But one day he overheard them talking, as they munched their new-baked oatcakes by the burn.

'Willie swims more like a selkie than a boy.'

'Maybe wee Willie is a selkie, Jessie.'

'Maybe he is.'

Willie came and sat down amongst them and began to eat his cake, and he thought of what they said. But he did not dare to ask a word about the selkies. And he wondered who his mother was and his father, where they were, and why he had lost them. He wondered until his head ached with it. And he wished he could find his mother and father.

Now the time drew on to midsummer, and the nights never grew dark in the islands, and many was the couple a-walking down the slopes in the summer twilight, who saw the wee grey folk, the trows who come on the hillside, moving in the shadows. Why, Jessie herself saw one, when she went up before sunrise to the pastures with the cows.

'I saw a wee old grey wife,' she said, 'lurking near the ring of rocks in the dawn glimmer. So I crossed myself quick, I said "God be about me", and at that minute the light of day welled up in the sky, and she was gone in a turn of the head.'

Well, now, wee Willie did not think much about the trows, nor the brownies either, who had to have their share when the harvest came, but he thought much about the selkies though he did not dare to ask about them.

When August came, then the boys were away with their father, to go to the Lammas fair at Kirkwall, and a young bullock with them and a pony.

'Well, Willie bairn, will you come with us or not?' said their father.

'I'll come with you,' said Willie, quickly. Now,

Willie could not have said why he wanted to go to the Lammas fair at all. But he had this feeling about it, that he must go, and maybe he would find out something important about himself.

'Now Willie, you must take these with you, woollen stockings and cloth to sell at the fair. Give them to father,' said his foster-mother, putting the things in a basket, as Willie prepared to run after the rest.

In they climbed and away they went, racing the other boats from the island, flying down the sounds until, before the day was over, they made Kirkwall.

And what with the people, and the cattle, and the horses, and the stalls Willie felt small and bewildered. He was standing by watching the farmers at their bargaining, when there was a tug at his sleeve and he turned to see a little girl, with a proud merry face.

'Have you ever seen the trows? Or the tangle? Or the nuggle, peerie face?' she whispered.

'Not I,' said Willie.

'I have seen them,' said she. 'Shall I tell you about them?'

'Not the trows,' said Willie scornfully, 'I know

enough about the trows, but have you seen the selkies?' he added.

'Oh the selkies!' said the maiden, 'I know all about the selkies.'

'What do you know?' said Willie quickly.

'They go up on the shore and be humans sometimes,' said she. 'And brave and handsome they are. My Mum has seen a selkie man. And if you want to speak to one of the selkie folk, you must drop seven tears in the water. And if a selkie loses his skin on the land, he cannot go back and dwell with his own folk.'

'What way would a selkie lose his skin?' said Willie.

'Folk might steal it.'

'But when could anybody take it?'

'When the selkies sit on the crags like humans, they put their skins beside them. I've got a selkie skin at home hanging up. Dad brought it off a stone by Ronaldsay. And it was so wee, Mum kept it.'

'Where's your home?' asked Willie, with his breath coming short, and his face glowing.

'Down there,' said she, pointing. 'Shall we play ball?'

'I'd rather see that selkie skin,' said Willie.

'Come on, then,' said the little girl, and off they ran.

'Mum,' said she, running into her home, 'here's a boy wants to see the selkie skin!' And she stood on a stool and hooked it off the peg.

27

'Where do you live, child?' said her mother. 'Haven't you ever seen the selkies?'

'I've seen the selkies all right,' said Willie. 'But will you give me this skin?'

'That old skin! Well, what can you give me for it?'

'An oatcake,' said Willie, looking in his pocket. The woman laughed.

'Take the skin, peerie face, and welcome,' she said, 'it'll make a cap for you, but it's so old.'

Willie was so pleased that he could only stand and stare and hug the selkie skin. Then he thanked the woman and ran away, and the little girl ran with him, and they played at rolling pebbles down the slopes.

And the next day, Willie's father was off home again before the folks were thick in the fair. He had sold the stockings and the wool and the bullock, and bought another pony and two geese, and there was Willie hugging tight to him his selkie skin. And never a word about it did he say, but took it home and hid it beneath his bed until morning.

Before the sunrise he was up out of his bed very softly, so as not to wake the others, and he was creeping out of the house with his selkie skin. Willie ran down the little slope with the air on his face cold and wet, and the dew crisp and silvery on the grass so that his feet left prints in it. First he found a round boulder, and pushed his selkie skin beneath it and covered it over to keep it safe, not knowing when he might want to use it. And then he ran on to the shore.

He threw off his clothes and he plunged into the green, pearly, early-morning sea, and out he swam to the selkies' rock, and reached it as the sun came tipping up from the far-off edge of the water. It was cold on the rock as he scrambled up, and he jumped to warm himself. And he pinched himself hard to make the tears come, but come they would not with that. So he thought of all the sad things he could, and last he thought of his mother and his father when they lost him. Seven tears slid out of Willie's eyes and dropped, plip, plop, into the water.

And then a wonderful thing happened. Up through the water the selkies came swimming, grey and shiny and silky. And two from the rest came near to the rock and lifted their heads and spoke to Willie.

'Bairn, bairn,' said his mother, for she it was, 'we've waited long and long for you, we've seen you on the ebb and upon the rocks, and never a word could we say, till you found out who you were.'

'Bairn, bairn,' said his father, for he it was, 'can't you find a selkie skin, and come back to your own folk?'

'We've been lonely without you.'

'Mother!' said Willie, 'Father!' he said, his face shining. 'I think I've found my own skin! My very own skin. It's under a stone on that hill!'

'Bring it, bring it, child,' said they joyfully, 'and we'll wait for you.'

Willie swam ashore, and he ran for his skin, a glistening little boy in the early sun, and he turned to the house and waved his hand.

'Fare you well, father, mother, and six bairns,' he cried. 'You've been good to me, but you are not like me. I am going back to my own folk!'

And he ran to the sea and dived from his rock, with his selkie skin about him, while the sun played music on the dimpled water, and the selkie folk turned and twisted in glee to meet him. And so little Willie found his mother and his father.

As for the good folk on the shore, some said he'd gone back to the trows. And some were afeared he was drowned. But the wisest said they always knew he was a selkie boy, who had lost his skin and was looking for it.

The Kitten Who Wanted
to be White

THERE was once a soot-black kitten called Tippety Witchet, who wanted nothing so much as she wanted to be white. As it was she was black all over from the tips of her ears to the spindly point of her tail, and the only things about her which were not black were her prickly pink tongue, as rough as a bread crust, and her sharp white teeth as pointed as a needle.

Now Tippety Witchet the black kitten looked at everything white, and the more she looked the more she wanted to be white herself. She pattered into the little girl's bedroom and saw the white curtains hanging there, so clean and crisp, and she coaxed them and clung to them until someone came and chased her away. Then she ran into the nursery and saw the baby's white ball, fresh and fluffy, and she frisked with it until she was tired. And she went into the kitchen next, and saw the white cups and plates, plain and polished, and up she jumped on to the dresser and went pitter patter over the piles of crockery, but never broke anything. And she went into the larder and saw the white morning milk, as smooth as silk, with the yellow cream on top. And she licked her black lips, but could not reach a drop.

'Oh my whiskers,' said the black kitten, 'how I wish I were white!' And she scuttled down the passage to watch for mice. They heard her coming and ran for their holes.

Tippety Witchet went into the garden to watch the cheeky birds. The sparrows on the roof puffed out their feathers and whispered 'Twittery-wittery, there goes Tippety', and the shiny great starlings pecked and hopped and squawked through the branches. And a very fat blackbird winked his eye at her.

'They all have black coats or brown coats or grey coats, and I don't care a button for them,' said Tippety. And she went to play with the clean white washing, billowing in the wind.

'Oh my whiskers,' sighed Tippety Witchet, 'how I wish I were as white as the washing!'

One day it was so cold and grey that everybody shivered and grumbled, and stamped their toes and blew their fingers. Tippety Witchet lay close inside, stretched out by the fire. The little boy and the little girl came home from school dancing with the cold.

'We shall have snow! We shall have snow!' they said as they danced.

'What is snow?' asked Tippety Witchet. But nobody answered, for nobody heard her, they were all so excited waiting for the snow. In the night it grew colder and colder, and Tippety Witchet crept up the stairs and went to sleep on the little girl's bed. And what should she see in the morning but the whole world white?

'Snow, snow, snow!' laughed the little girl, waking up. Tippety Witchet jumped on to the window-sill and sat watching the wisps of twirling, curling, falling snow. The house was white and the trees were white, the garden was white and the road was white, and the steeple and the people, and the school and the hall, the hedges and the ledges, and every narrow edge, everything was as white as the kitten wished to be.

'Oh my whiskers,' said Tippety Witchet, 'I'm going out to get white.'

In the garden the hungry birds were hopping around in the snow, eating the food from the plate some kind person put out. There were chaffinches and other finches, blue tits and other tits, speckled thrushes, fat blackbirds, red robins, and plenty of sparrows and starlings. But what the kitten liked most were the great white seagulls who came in from the cold grey sea, and frightened all the others. Soon the kitten was as white as they, but when she went in to show how proud she was, her white coat melted, and she was only very wet.

'Bother,' said Tippety, 'I shall go out and stay out.' And she rolled and frisked in the lovely snow. She went to see the Christmas tree, planted in the garden, and all its tinkling balls and bells put away for another year. But now it had white gloves on every hand, and looked even prettier, covered with the spangled snow. Tippety Witchet patted it and watched the white snow fall, so soft and sparkling.

'Will you keep your white coat for ever?' asked the kitten.

'Not when it thaws,' whispered the Christmas tree.

'What is thaw?' asked Tippety Witchet.

'You'll see soon enough,' said the little Christmas tree.

Tippety Witchet went round to the front of the house, and there on the lawn were three people instead of two: the little boy, the little girl, and a person in a white, white coat.

'Oh my whiskers, who's this?' said the kitten jumping round.

'Our snowman,' said the little girl.

'Where did he come from?' said Tippety Witchet.

'We made him,' said the little boy, and they went off to play snowballs.

'Where did you really come from?' said Tippety Witchet to the snowman.

But the snowman just stood, thinking cold thoughts. The kitten went a bit nearer.

'Where are you when you're not in the garden?' she said.

'Nowhere,' said the snowman.

'Where is Nowhere?' said the little kitten.

'Where the winds live, and the clouds and the frost and the rain and the hail and the snow,' said the snowman.

'Does the sun shine there?' asked Tippety.

'Oh yes,' said the snowman, 'bright as the buttons on the little boy's coat and much brighter.

Golden as the hair under the little girl's cap, and much shinier.'

'Do all the people have white coats in No-where?' said the kitten.

'Yes, indeed,' said the snowman.

'Then will you take me when you go back?' said Tippety Witchet.

'Are you wise?' said the snowman.

'I don't care about being wise,' said the kitten, 'as long as I am white.'

'We are all wise in Nowhere because we look at the snow all day, which is as wise and white as a new world.'

'Very well, I don't mind being wise, too,' said the kitten.

'Then come into the garden at midnight,' said the snowman, 'and you shall come with me.'

That night the moon was bewitchingly bright on the cold snow, and the whole world looked wise and white. Tippety waited till midnight, and then she heard tinkle twinkle, spinkle spankle, ding dong derry, merry little bells. She jumped out of the kitchen window into the moony garden, and there was Snowman sitting in a chariot, pulled

with white horses made of cloudiness, and jingling bells all round. So in jumped Tippety and off they went to Nowhere.

Next morning, there was only a lump that the snowman had stood on.

'The snowman's gone,' called the little boy.

'Where is Tippety Witchet?' asked the little girl. And nobody could find her. They went round the garden, looking in the corners.

'Tippety, Tippety, where are you?'

'She's gone with the snowman,' said the little Christmas tree. 'I saw them go in the moonlight.'

'Oh dear,' said the little girl, 'I hope she'll get back safely.'

That evening at milk-time, five o'clock tea time, in came a little white kitten like Tippety.

'You're not Tippety Witchet,' said the little boy.

'Yes I am,' said Tippety wisely.

'Where have you been?' asked the little girl.

'Nowhere,' said puss. 'I went with Snowman.' And she frisked about the kitchen in her snow-white coat, so glad to be white that there was no holding her.

'Well, I never,' said the little boy, as he stroked

her, 'you're as white as the icing was, upon the Christmas cake.'

And that was how Tippety Witchet got white.

The Boy Who Ran Away

THERE was once a little boy who was walking in the park, kicking at his toes and looking for adventures. He did not like his mother holding his hand, and he did not like his sister because everybody noticed her as she sat in her pram and waved her rattle.

Now they had not gone very far when they came to the pond with ducks floating on it, and everybody watching them. The little boy's mother also stopped to watch them, and then by chance let go of his hand.

'Aha!' thought the little boy, 'now I'll run away.'

So he took to his heels and he ran and he ran. He had not gone very far before he met a scooter, a bright yellow scooter, scooting up the paths on its bright red wheels.

'Hey!' said the little boy. 'Where are you going?'

'I'm going for a scoot. Would you like to come with me?'

'Yes,' said the little boy, and off they scooted.

They hadn't gone far before they met a tricycle, a bright blue tricycle pedalling up the pathway.

'Hey!' said the little boy, 'where are you going? I ran away from mummy until I met this scooter.'

'Oh,' said the tricycle, 'I'm going to meet a friend of mine. Want to come with me?'

'Yes,' said the little boy, and off they pedalled.

They hadn't gone far before they met a bicycle, a black and silver bicycle, ringing its bell.

'Hey!' said the little boy, 'where are you going? I ran away from mummy until I met a scooter. And I scooted on the scooter until I met a tricycle.'

'I see,' said the bicycle, putting both its brakes on. 'I'm going for a fast spin. Like to come with me?'

'Yes,' said the little boy. So off they bicycled.

They pedalled and they pedalled to the top of a steep hill, and flew down at a great rate not pedalling at all.

'Phew!' said the little boy, 'that was lovely!'

They hadn't gone far when they met a new motor-car, a brand new motor-car, hooting on its hooter.

'Hey!' said the little boy, 'where are you off to? I ran away from mummy until I met a scooter, and I scooted on the scooter until I met a tricycle, and I pedalled on the tricycle until I met this bicycle.'

'Ha, ha!' said the motor-car, 'I'm going for a joy-ride. Care to come with me, on my new leather cushions?'

'Yes,' said the little boy, climbing in eagerly. So off they went, with the road spinning under them.

They hadn't gone far, when they overtook an omnibus, a great red omnibus with a great gloomy face.

'If you want to go farther, just whistle to that omnibus, because this is where I live,' said the brand new motor-car.

'Hey!' said the little boy, 'where are you heading for? I ran away from mummy until I met a scooter, and I scooted on the scooter until I met a tricycle, and I pedalled on the tricycle until I met a bicycle, and I cycled on the bicycle until I met that motor-car.'

'Humph!' said the omnibus, 'I'm going to the country. If you want to come with me, you'd better get aboard.'

'All right,' said the little boy, jumping on the omnibus, and off went the omnibus climbing up a hill.

It groaned and it grumbled and then it started
humming, and then it sang right up the scale and
had to start again.

Now, they'd gone a good distance when they
saw a green engine puffing and panting along a
railway bridge.

'This is where I stop,' said the bus to the little

boy. 'You'd better catch that train if you're going on again.'

'Hi!' said the little boy, 'where are you making for? I ran away from mummy until I met a scooter and I scooted on the scooter until I met a tricycle, and I pedalled on the tricycle until I met a bicycle, and I cycled on the bicycle until I met a motor-car, and I whizzed off in the motor-car until I met this omnibus.'

'Pouff!' said the green train, taking its top hat off, 'I'm going to the sea-side, much faster than a bus. Jump in if you want to, I haven't time to dally.'

'Rather,' said the little boy, and scrambled up the engine, and off went the haughty train:

'Pouff! pouff! pouff!'

They panted through the countryside with

smoke curling round them, until at last the little boy spied the great sea.

'I don't cross the channel, though I could if I wanted to! Pouff!' said the green train, 'I don't like the sea. If you want to go over, you'd better hail a steamer. They're rather large and vulgar things, if you ask me. And not content with one top hat, they flourish two or three.'

'Ahoy!' said the little boy, waving to a steamer, 'where are you sailing to, I'd like to know? I ran away from mummy until I met a scooter, and I scooted on the scooter until I met a tricycle, and I pedalled on the tricycle until I met a bicycle, and I cycled on the bicycle until I met a motor-car, and I whizzed off in the motor-car until I met an omnibus, and I jolted in the omnibus until I met an engine.'

'Hoots!' said the steamer, 'I'm sailing to the Continent. If you want to come too, I'll let down the gangway.'

'I do,' said the little boy, and ran aboard the ship.

'Hoo–oots!' said the steamer dipping through the water, and it wasn't very long before they reached the other side.

Now just as they were docking they saw a silver aeroplane.

'There,' boomed the steamer, 'you'd better catch that.'

'Hullo–o!' cried the little boy, putting both his hands up. 'Where are you flying to next, if you please? I ran away from mummy until I met a scooter and I scooted on the scooter until I met a tricycle, I pedalled on the tricycle until I met a bicycle, and I cycled on the bicycle until I met a motor-car. I whizzed off in the motor-car until I met an omnibus: I jolted in the omnibus until I met an engine, and I panted in the engine until I met a steamer.'

'M-m-m-m-m,' said the aeroplane. 'I'm going back to England. Want to come with me?'

'Yes, please,' said the little boy, and clambered up the steps.

'M-m-m-mind,' said the aeroplane, climbing up the cloud banks. 'Put your head inside, or you'll lose it in the clouds.'

They went so fast they were back in a twinkling and landed at the aerodrome about five o'clock.

On his way home the little boy saw a postman, standing in the street with a sack on his back.

'I say!' said the little boy, 'where are you going? I ran away from mummy until I met a scooter and I scooted on the scooter until I met a tricycle, and I pedalled on the tricycle until I met a bicycle, and I cycled on the bicycle until I met a motor-car. I whizzed off in the motor-car until I met an omnibus, I jolted in the omnibus until I met an engine, and I panted in the engine until I met a steamer, and I sailed off in the steamer until I met an aeroplane.'

'Umph!' said the postman, putting his sack down. 'I am the postman delivering the last post.'

'Oh?' said the little boy. 'Do you go near Croydon?'

'Yes,' said the postman, 'I know where you live. Hop in the sack and I'll give you a ride.'

So they walked till they came to a house in Croydon, with a fence around it and a garden in the front.

'Now,' said the postman, 'I'll knock on the door knocker, and when the door opens, out you jump.'

So the little boy got ready, laughing in his coat sleeve, and the postman knocked: 'Rat a tat tat!'

And when the door opened, the postman said,

'A parcel.' And out jumped the little boy: 'Bo! bo! bo! I ran away from mummy until I met a scooter and I scooted on the scooter until I met a tricycle and I pedalled on the tricycle until I met a bicycle and I cycled on the bicycle until I met a motor-car. I whizzed off in the motor-car until I met an omnibus, and I jolted in the omnibus until I met an engine, I panted in the engine until I met a steamer, and I sailed off in the steamer until I met an aeroplane, I floated in the aeroplane until I met the postman! AND HE'S

BROUGHT ME WITH THE LETTERS IN THE VERY
LAST POST!'

So they thanked the postman kindly and said,
'Good-evening.' And the little boy was very glad
to see all his family, and the family were very glad
to see the little boy. And as he was so hungry, they
gave him lots of supper. He had all the things he
liked the best before he went to bed.

The Cat and the Fiddle

ONCE upon a time when cats were cleverer than they are now, there lived in a tidy little cattery a widow cat and her three clever kittens.

Now the eldest kitten was black as coal, and very vain indeed. And the second cat was a cyprus-cat, which means she had tabby stripes.

And the third kitten was round like an orange and coloured like an orange, and his name was Tangerine.

Their mamma had not much money, and a very hard job it was to keep going. So she used to grow radishes behind the cattery and sell them for three-pence the bunch to other cats. When she asked the kittens to help tie the bunches, they all said something different.

The black kitten said: 'Shan't. I'm greasing my whiskers.'

The tabby kitten said: 'Can't. I'm combing my fur.'

But the youngest tangerine kitten said: 'Very well, Mamma, I'm just coming,' and scampered off to help her.

Inside the cattery were three little baskets belonging to the three kittens; but their poor dear mamma had to sleep on the hearth rug. And on the rug were three little plates belonging to the three kittens, but their poor dear mamma used to eat off the floor.

And the bigger the kittens grew, the more they used to eat, and the less there was left for their poor mamma. In the end they grew so poor, radishes or no radishes, that she did not know what to do. Now it happened that by this time the coal black kitten, who was so very vain, was nearly grown-up.

'Black kitten,' said his mamma to him, 'you must go out into the world and make your fortune. And when you have made it, remember your sister and brother and your poor dear mamma and come back.'

'Very well,' said the black kitten, twirling his long whiskers, 'but what in the cattery can I take with me? I can't go and seek my fortune with nothing.'

So his mamma looked about and she saw in the cupboard his dear papa's black silk top hat. And also his spotted cravat.

'Here,' she said, 'is a black silk hat and a spotted cravat. They will suit you very well.'

The kitten was pleased, and put them on, and cut himself a cane from a raspberry bush. Then off he went down the cattery path, waving at his sister and brother and his poor dear mamma, and determined to seek his fortune.

He walked and he walked until he came to London, and there he met a gentleman walking down the Mall. He had black hair and whiskers and a top hat just like the cat, and carried a cane in his hand.

'There,' said the kitten, 'I should like him for my master: a real rich gentleman in a black silk hat.'

When the gentleman saw the kitten with a hat like his own, he was very pleased and flattered. So they fixed it up between them, the kitten and the gentleman. The kitten wore white spats, and joined the Kit Cat Club, and forgot his dear mamma.

So the days went by, and the kitten never came, so his sister and his brother and his poor mamma stopped hoping, and said: 'He must have found a master.' Which was very true.

Then her mamma said to the second kitten: 'Cyprus kitten, you must go and seek your fortune, and when you have made it, remember your brother and your poor dear mamma.'

'Very well,' said the kitten who was nearly grown-up. 'But may I have something to take with me on my travels? I cannot earn my fortune with nothing at all.'

So her mamma looked about all round the cattery, and she found nothing at all but her next-to-best bonnet.

'Here,' said she, 'you may have this bonnet with blue silk ribbons. It will suit you very well.'

The cyprus kitten was delighted, and put on the bonnet, and picked herself a blue flower to wear behind her ear. Then off she went down the cattery path, blowing kisses to her brother and her dear, kind mamma.

When she reached a signpost which said London, she turned around and went another way.

'I don't like London,' said the cyprus kitten. 'I shall go to the country instead, to seek my fortune.'

She had not gone very far when she came to a cottage, a sweet, neat, enticing cottage with lavender and catmint growing in the beds, and roses under the windows.

'That's the very place for me,' said the cyprus kitten. 'I wonder who lives there?'

She went up to the door and rattled the handle, tittle-tattle with her paw. There came to the door a little old woman, in a next-to-best-bonnet with purple ribbons.

'Well!' she said, shaking her ribbons, 'a sleek, streaky kitten in a bonnet like mine!' And she asked the kitten in. And when they found they liked each other, they arranged to live together. And the cyprus kitten, like her black brother, forgot all about her brother Tangerine and her mamma.

And mamma and the tangerine kitten waited. But the cyprus kitten did not come back, so they very sensibly said to each other: 'I expect

she has found a mistress.' Which was exactly
true.

'Tangerine kitten,' said her poor dear mamma,
'you will have to go now, and seek your
fortune, and what I shall do without you I do
not know.'

Now the tangerine kitten comforted his mamma, and promised that he would not be long in
making his fortune.

'Then,' said he, 'I shall come back and fetch
you, and we shall live very happily together ever
after. But is there anything I can take to earn my
fortune?'

His mamma looked about, and she could not
find anything to give to the tangerine kitten for
his fortune. But just as they were giving up hope,
she found an old fiddle at the back of the cupboard.

'Here,' said she, 'is a very old fiddle. Perhaps
you could play it.'

'The older the better,' said the wise little kitten.
'I have always wanted a fiddle.'

So he kissed his mamma, and took his fiddle,
and went off down the cattery path to seek his
fortune.

Now the first thing he did was to learn to play the fiddle, which was hard for a kitten. But he practised and practised, and as he was a musical kitten, he soon began to learn. He played 'Hey diddle diddle', and 'Hickory dickory dock', and 'Humpty dumpty', and many other tunes.

He slept in barns and haystacks, and practised in the moonlight.

Now, one fine day, not long after he had left, he came to a village green with a maypole in the middle. All round the maypole pretty girls were gathering, but nobody could dance as there wasn't a fiddler.

'Aha!' thought the tangerine kitten, who was hiding in some trees. 'Here is my chance to make my fortune.' So he went up with his fiddle, and said politely to the people: 'I could play your music, for a very modest fee.'

'A cat and a fiddle!' said the girls. 'Let's try him!'

So the kitten fiddled and the people danced, until they were all worn out.

'Will you stay with us, and be the village fiddler?' said the girls to the kitten.

'Certainly,' said he, 'but I must have a house for two, and I must go and fetch my mamma.'

So he went off again to fetch his mamma. And they both went to live in a cosy cattery made for them near the village green. As the kitten earned his fortune by being a fiddler, his poor dear mamma did not have to grow radishes. She grew catmint and lavender instead.

The Musical-Box

THERE was once a little musical-box made of the finest gold which gleamed like the sunshine and was enamelled with the tiniest, prettiest flowers which had eyes like jewels.

It had been made by an old pedlar who had a great eye for a pretty thing, and he kept it always in his pocket, to give himself a tune as he plodded along the weary roads.

But there came a winter when the poor pedlar was ill, and could no longer travel from town to town, and from park to palace selling his pretty things. He lay in a poor room, cold and hungry, and was forced to sell all he had to buy himself food.

In the end he had to sell the musical-box. He sold it to a toymaker who lived in the town; he sold it for the money it would fetch.

'Never fear, little box,' said the pedlar, as he parted from it. 'As soon as I am well again, I will come to the toymaker and buy you back. For I hardly suppose he will sell you here, so pretty and expensive you are to be sure.'

So the musical-box stood on the shelf of the toymaker's shop. And although it was sad to part from the master who made it, it said to itself nevertheless as it waited:

'Tinkle-tank! This is an adventure! Who knows, twinkle-tee, how lucky I may be, where I may go and who'll buy me! I will sing my best to everyone who comes, for I am the prettiest, daintiest, merriest, tinkle-tee, tankle-tee, musical-box!'

And so when the toymaker played it to the people who came in, its tunes were the merriest you could wish to hear, like the tunes that water sings.

'Ah,' sighed the people, 'it is indeed the loveliest musical-box! But we cannot afford to buy it, that we can't. Why, it would cost a king's ransom.'

So the little musical-box stayed in the shop waiting.

Now, one day there came into the toymaker's shop a very grand person, all ribbons and rosettes. And he said:

'Mr Toymaker, it is the Princess's birthday, and the King has sent me to buy a present. It must be a pretty present, a costly present, and the kind of present the Princess would approve. What have you to show me?'

'Has she a doll?' asked the toymaker.

'Ten thousand,' said the Chamberlain.

'Has she a dolls' house?' asked the toymaker.

'More than many,' said the Chamberlain, 'and all furnished.'

'Has she books?' asked the toymaker.

'A whole room full,' said the Chamberlain.

'Has she stuffed animals?'

'Enough for a zoo,' said the Chamberlain and yawned.

'Then what has she *not*?' asked the toymaker.

'Nothing that I know of,' replied the Chamberlain. 'The Princess has everything she wants.' And he yawned again.

'Has she a musical-box?' asked the toymaker eagerly.

'Not a single one, that I have ever seen,' cried the Chamberlain in quite a different voice, and he stopped yawning at once.

'Here is the best musical-box you could wish to see,' said the toymaker. 'But it is very expensive. I had it from an old pedlar who made it himself. And he said, had he not been starving, he would never have sold it, so charming and pretty it is.'

'Does it sing well?' asked the Chamberlain.

'Like a nightingale,' said the toymaker.

'Then we will have it. The King will be delighted to find something the Princess does not already possess in hundreds,' said the Chamberlain. And he laid down some golden coins and took the little musical-box away.

'A princess! A princess!' tinkled the box to itself, in his pocket. 'How fine I shall be living with a princess!'

Now, at first the Princess was delighted with the musical-box, for she had never in her life seen one. She kissed it and played it and thought it the merriest thing she had ever heard.

T–BTG–C

'Merrily, merrily, merry as birds I be,' laughed the musical-box.

And it was so pleased to belong to someone again that it sang its very best for the Princess and never tired.

Its handle grew dizzy and its poor little voice quite sore, but still it sang and sang as she played it. For it was a cheerful and loving musical-box, and wished to please.

But the trouble with that Princess was that she was spoilt. She had so many toys, and so many dolls and so much of everything that she soon grew tired of one thing and went on to the next. And the little musical-box was stuffed away in the back of a cupboard underneath other things which were all broken and sad. Nobody played it and it grew lonely, and began to wish it were still with its kind master, the pedlar.

'Lackaday, lackadee, nobody plays with me,
   Tunes do grow rusty so, lackadaydee,'
sighed the little box.

And one day the nurse found it, pushed away in the cupboard.

'What is this that you never play with?' said she.

The Princess played it for the last time. But the musical-box could only sing a plaintive tune, because it felt wounded in its heart.

'It is too dreary,' said the Princess, and she gave it to her lady-in-waiting.

'Come,' thought the box to itself, 'this is better than being shut in a cupboard!'

And the lady-in-waiting said: 'This *was* a fine little musical-box before that spoilt Princess chipped it and bent it until there are no flowers left. Let us see how it sings.'

The musical-box sighed and did its best, though it could not help but be sorry about its flowers and its shape. And so its tune was sad and slow.

'Tinkle-tee!' whispered the box, 'My tunes come all tangled, my music is jangled, my flowers so spangled are broken and dim.'

The lady-in-waiting kept it for a while amongst the bottles and bowls on her dressing table. But she never played it, for she cared nothing for tunes, and did not sing herself. The musical-box grew tired of looking at the bottles and the silver brushes, and wished it were anywhere but there. And one day the lady-in-waiting gave it to the kitchen maid.

'Tinkle-tay!' sighed the musical-box. 'Better be used in the kitchen than neglected on the dressing table!' And it hoped for better things.

Now the kitchen maid was very set up and said to the rest:

'Look what I've got! A musical-box!'

'It is tarnished and rather ugly,' said they, 'but let us see how it plays.'

The little musical-box was stiff, stiff with not being played for many a day. And it was ashamed to think it was tarnished and ugly.

'Tarnished!' it sighed. 'They say I am tarnished! I used to be golden, but I have grown old.'

So although it tried its hardest, its tune came out far from merry.

'What a dismal thing!' said the kitchen maid. And she stuffed it into the shoe cupboard. The musical-box was battered and dirty and covered with dust.

'Jingle-jangle,' it whispered, 'tattered and battered and tinny am I.' And it felt sad.

One day the Boots found it as he was cleaning the shoes.

'What have *I* found?' said he. 'It's a dirty old musical-box! We'll see how it plays.'

And he tried to turn the handle. But the handle was so bent and the musical-box so rusty, that it could only sing the poorest of tunes, and so slowly, that the boot-boy laughed.

He pulled and pushed, but he was not clever enough to mend it, so he threw it out into the yard where it fell with a tin-tan-tangle on the stones. The little musical-box groaned and lay waiting.

There came a pedlar along one day to the palace, and he went to the back door to sell his knacks and pretties to the servants. He had ribbons and brooches and laces and combs and a hundred other things. And as he turned away from the door, he saw the musical-box.

'Hey, Boots!' cried he to the boot-boy. 'May I take this musical-box?'

'For aught I care,' said Boots. 'It is no good at all.'

'We will see,' said the pedlar smiling. And he picked it carefully up, and dusted it, for he had an eye for pretty things. And as he walked along the road he tried to turn the handle, but the weary musical-box could not sing a single note.

'Come, now, my pretty little box,' said the pedlar kindly, 'try what you can do. But first I will wash you, to make you feel better.'

And he took the box to a stream and washed its outside carefully with his handkerchief. The sun came out and caught it in a golden gleam.

'That's better,' said the pedlar, 'I believe you are a golden box.' And he polished and rubbed. 'Why, bless my soul,' said he, as he rubbed a little harder, 'I believe you are my very own box, for I can see the flowers upon you which I painted myself! Come, now, can you not sing for your master?'

'Twinkle-tee' said the musical-box to itself. 'I believe it *is* my master.' And it took heart again and gathered up its strength and sang, very slowly and rather wearily to the pedlar.

'Splendid!' cried the pedlar. 'My own dear little box! I will put you right in a twinkling!'

And he took the musical-box home. He cleaned it and oiled it and straightened it, and then he painted it with flowers again until it looked like itself.

'There!' said he, when it was done, 'I will never sell you again, not as long as I live.'

'Tinkle-tee! How merry I be!' said the musical-box, when it heard this, for it had had more than enough of being sold, the poor little thing.

And that night after the pedlar was in bed, there began the most delightful music, spinkle and spankle all through the pedlar's room.

It was the musical-box.

The pedlar opened one eye. 'You can sing of your own accord, can you, my pretty?' said the pedlar.

'That I can,' said the musical-box, 'since you found me again. I am the happiest, luckiest, merriest, daintiest, prettiest musical-box!'

And it sang its master to sleep with a song as merry as a black-bird in a cherry tree.

A Christmas Story

IT was a clear and frosty Christmas Eve. All day long the people in the busy streets had been going back and forth with their baskets and their parcels, their turkeys and their Christmas trees.

All the gay shops stayed open late, and the men on the pavements sold hopping monkeys and glittering balls, toys for girls and treasures for boys. And the street lamps came on over the city and glowed with a halo of light, making pools of brightness on the pavements. The taxis stopped and started, the glittering buses fully of happy people made their way through the cars and the crowds, until it grew very late, and most folk were at home by their fire-sides, and most children in bed with a stocking at their feet.

Not many people had been to the Zoo that day. They were all too busy making their mince-pies or hanging up their holly. It was too cold, they thought, to tramp slowly round looking at the creatures. Only a few keepers were there, blowing upon their fingers to keep the frost out, stamping their toes and beating their arms. They went home early, to join in the fun, and all the animals, fed and warm in their houses, settled down for the night. And then a strange thing happened.

It all began in the corner of a barn where straw was stacked, warm and dry, ready to be put in the creatures' cages. In this straw lived families of rats, with sharp eyes and long whiskers. There were several fathers and several mothers and a great many children who were romping and chasing in the barn.

'Shall I tell you,' said an old grey rat, as he sat stroking his whiskers, 'what I heard, as the keepers talked, gathering up the clean straw?'

'By all means, let me hear,' said his wife.

'They were going home to a party,' said he, 'of

all their friends. And there were to be good things to eat and drink and games and talk, and bright fires, and all because it is Christmas Eve.'

'Let *us* have a party! Let *us* have games and good things to eat!' said the young rats, scampering up as they heard him speak.

'If it is Christmas Eve,' said one, 'let's ask all our friends!'

'Let's call on the mice,' said another.

'I am fond of the guinea-pigs,' said a third.

'My favourite animal is the elephant,' said a very small rat; 'he lets me pick up the pieces in his house whenever I like.'

'If we are going to ask the elephant,' said the first old rat, 'we shall not be able to have our party in *this* barn. It is too full of straw, and the elephant is a large animal.'

'I don't think,' said a mild matronly rat, 'that we can ask the elephant and not the lions, or the giraffe, or the hippopotamus. It would be very unkind.'

'It is clear that we must ask them all,' said a wise rat from the window ledge. 'Feathered or furred, stiff or sleek, smooth or bristled, we must ask them *all* to our party.'

'It is a bright, clear night, and the stars are out,' said his companion on the ledge, looking from the window. 'Let's have the party outside, and then there will be room for every animal in the Zoo.'

'Hurrah, hurrah! Let's have them *all*!' squeaked the young rats in their excitement.

To this plan they agreed, and while the rest began to collect the food, the smallest rat hurried off to be messenger and to visit every house in the Zoo.

All was still under the dark blue sky. The smallest rat hurried to the elephant's house, found his way in by his usual hole, and crept between the bars.

'Elephant,' said he, scampering up the beast's leathery back and whispering in his ear, 'are you asleep?'

The elephant flicked his flappy ear and opened one eye.

'It is you, little rat,' he said, 'you can have whatever you can find.' And he went back to sleep again.

'But, Elephant,' said the rat, 'I have come to invite you to a party. It is Christmas Eve.'

'O-ho,' said the elephant sleepily. 'It is very

kind of you, but I'm afraid I couldn't leave my house tonight. I seldom go out without a keeper. Where is your party?'

'It is to be outside, under the sky,' said the little rat. 'Do come Elephant, if you can,' said he, 'because it's Christmas Eve.' And he ran off to tell the brown bears.

The brown bears were asleep in their pit with only the tips of their ears showing.

'Bears,' said the rat, 'are you awake?'

There was no answer, only a regular fluffy snore, snore.

'Bears,' said the rat, more loudly, tweaking their furry ears, 'I have come to invite you to our party.'

'It is very kind of you, rat,' said the sleepy bears, 'but I don't think it would be warm enough for us to come out of our houses tonight. We'll see how we feel in half-an-hour's time.'

And they rolled over and were soon snoring again.

The rat hurried on to where the lions lived, and slid between the great bars, with his heart in his mouth. For he was always a little afraid of the lions' paws. The great yellow lion was still awake, and he yawned and flickered his eyelids.

'Hullo, small animal,' said he, 'what brings you to *my* house on this cold and frosty night when most folk are in bed?'

'Lion,' said the rat, feeling very small, and his voice right up in the air with fright, 'it is Christmas Eve, and we are having a party, for us all. We shouldn't be happy unless you, the King of beasts, were there. Please come, Sir, if you can.'

'It is good of you to invite me, small animal,' replied the lion, 'but I doubt if I shall be able to manage it tonight. For, to tell you the truth, I have put away the key of my cage and can't think where to look for it. But I wish you a very happy time.'

The little rat felt sad that none of the animals could come to the party. But he trotted away to the polar bears, and the mountain goats, and the sea lions and the penguins.

'We should find it rather a long way to come,' said the polar bears, politely.

'We will come if we are awake!' barked the sea lions.

'Thank you very much,' sniffed the young penguins, when they awoke, 'but we all have colds.'

'O dear,' sighed the rat, 'why do they all make excuses?' And off he ran to the giraffes and the hippopotamus and the rhinoceros, and the camels, and the monkeys, and the zebra, and the deer and all the birds, and even the snakes, and invited them all to the party. But wherever he went, it was the same. They were all very kind and polite; but they all made excuses.

Last of all, the little rat went to the donkeys and scampered up to their great, fluffy ears as they lay on the ground.

'I should love to go,' said the youngest donkey, jumping to his feet. 'I should *so* love to go.' And he brayed with pleasure.

'I'm afraid you can't,' said his mother.

'But it's Christmas Eve,' pleaded the rat. 'Surely you can come? Please do,' he went on, 'for everyone makes excuses, and we shall be disappointed if *no one* comes to our party!'

And he shed a tear or two.

'Kind rat,' said the donkey, 'it is not that we should not like to. But we cannot. . . . It is rather hard to explain – we cannot, you see, *get out of our houses*,' she whispered in a low voice, looking very ashamed.

And then the poor rat understood. He ran back to the rest, and told his tale.

'And I'm afraid,' he said, 'that nobody at all will come, not because they would not like to, but because they *cannot get out of their houses.*'

So the rats and mice comforted themselves as best they could by beginning to have their party alone.

Meanwhile, the friendly elephant, turning over in his sleep, dreamed that his cage stood open on this frosty night, and that he went to the party. And he woke up with a start, and looked about him.

'Well,' he muttered, 'it can do no harm to try. I have not rattled my door for a long time.'

And he walked over to the front of his house, lifted his trunk, tried the latches, and lo and behold, the doors were all open! So he strode out, bellowing through his trunk for joy as he walked to the party.

And the lions in their houses woke up and thought of the rat and his invitation, and slinking up to their doors they lifted their strong pads to the latches. And they were all open! So out came the lions and the lionesses, the tigers and the leopards, the pumas and the giant panda. And they were all as meek and mild as lambs because it was Christmas Eve. Sniffing the bright frosty air, they padded off to the party.

Then the agile monkeys and the long-necked giraffes, the humpy camels, the polar bears, the goats, the sea lions, the penguins, the hippos and the rhinos, the naughty striped zebra, the deer, the oxen and the gentle donkeys, the birds and the snakes and the insects, the wild dogs, and all the beasts, feathered and furred, striped and spotted, finding themselves free, came quietly out to the party, and all so gently that they were not afraid of each other.

When the rats heard the sound of the feet, hoofed and padded, and many wings whirring, they were delighted.

'Listen!' said they, pricking up their ears, 'it's the birds and animals coming to the party!'

And they scampered to meet them.

And then the revels began. The giraffe stood with his long neck bent to the earth while the rats and the guinea-pigs and all the little animals played at sliding down it. And the elephant lifted the adventurous young goats, the lambs and the

tiger cubs, and gave them swings on his trunk. And the lions and tigers and leopards ran races and leapt about up and down, up and down the gravel paths. And the polar bears begged and did their tricks. And the camels gave rides to all who asked. And the gentle donkeys trotted round with the smallest apes on their backs, holding on to their stiff manes.

When all the animals were tired, they sat in a ring while the happy rats handed round the good things they had collected. The stars twinkled brightly in the sky, and the frost sparkled on the grass.

'It is very cold,' said the smallest lamb to the furry lion, 'do you think I might sit between your paws?'

'By all means, little lamb,' said the largest lion, licking the tiny creature's head.

'Let us tell stories under the stars,' said the antelope.

'Yes, let's tell stories!' squeaked the youngest rats.

'I'll begin,' said the old grey rat who had first thought of the party. 'Long ago,' he said, 'in a far-off land, on this very night, which is Christmas, there was a human child born. But not in a house and a bed. In a stable in straw, like us. And a special bright star shone because of him.'

'How do you know these things?' said some of the others.

'The story is handed down from my ancestors,' said the old rat. 'Some of them lived in that stable, and peeped out and saw the little child. But it is a long, weary time ago. Soon afterwards, the rats boarded a boat at the Palestine coast, loaded with dyes and spices, and came to live in this land.'

'Yes,' said the donkeys, 'we know that story is true. It is told in our family how the child was put in the manger, and some of us stood by. And some

of us carried his mother; and some himself, when he was a man.'

'We were there too,' said the great oxen. 'We warmed the child with our breath.'

'We were the first to see the star,' said the lamb, from between the lion's paws, 'and hear the angels singing.'

'I gave him my strength,' said the lion.

'We gave him our gentleness,' cooed the doves, from the roof where they sat.

'He has our wisdom,' said the serpents.

'As for me,' said the great fawn camel, 'I taught him how to kneel to carry his burdens. But the burdens he carried were always heavier than mine.'

Across the frosty air came the clamour of the midnight bells, swinging and rejoicing from the churches of the people. And the animals kneeled in their ring.

The next day, when the keepers came, blowing their nails, into the straw barn, one said to another:

'Did you see the way the gravel is turned up, down there in the main walk?'

'I did,' said the other. 'Anyone would think the gardeners had had a holiday.'

'It looks to me,' said his friend, 'as if the animals had a party!'

And they both laughed, heaving the warm, dry straw.

But the rats, hiding in their corner, said nothing.

The Walking Stick

ONCE there was an old
baron who lived in an old
castle in the ancient kingdom of Tiddleywinks.
Now the old baron
thought he would like to
end his days peacefully
sitting in his armchair in
his own bedroom at the
top of three hundred stairs in the
castle turrets.

'I am too old,' said he, stroking
his silvery beard which wandered
to his ankles, 'and too stiff,' said
he, stretching his old legs out to
the fire, 'and altogether too lazy,'
said he, yawning so wide that his
nightcap fell off, 'to do any more
work in the kingdom of Tiddley-
winks. I shall call my three sons and share my
wealth out between them. Then I shall have my

meals on a tray to avoid going up and down the three hundred stairs, and I shall take the air on my own turret battlements.'

So he called to his three sons, and they came, puff, pant, puff, pant, up the three hundred stairs and arrived at the top a trifle out of breath.

'Now, my dears,' said the old baron, 'I am too old and too stiff and altogether too lazy to do any more work. So I shall share out my wealth and my work between you, and I shall stay up here and have all my meals on a tray.'

'Very well, father,' said the three sons. 'We will do as you say.'

The eldest was a tall dark fellow with a face as purple as a plum (but perhaps that was the three hundred stairs). The second was a tall fair lad with hair as straight as a straw thatch, and a sly look. The third was smaller and merrier, and altogether pleasanter. Their names were Noughts-and-Crosses, Snakes-and-Ladders, and Jigsaw.

'Now, you, Noughts-and-Crosses,' said the old baron, 'shall look after the animals of the castle farm, and that shall be your portion.'

'But I don't know anything about animals, and

neither do I care a jot,' said Noughts-and-Crosses, crossly.

'Then you shall learn,' said his father. 'And you, Snakes-and-Ladders,' said he, turning to his second son, 'shall look after the fields and the orchard and sell the food to the villagers, and that shall be your portion.'

'But I don't know anything of apples and barley-corn, and I do not care a fig for the villagers,' said Snakes-and-Ladders, slyly.

'Then you must learn,' said the baron. 'And you, my merry Jigsaw, all there is for you to do is to help your brothers. Neither have I anything to give you except this walking-stick.' And he handed him a walking-stick, smooth and brown, with an ivory handle. And the ivory handle had a face carved on it, merry and bland, and so alive that it looked at you.

Now, at this Noughts-and-Crosses snorted and nudged his second brother, and Snakes-and-Ladders smiled and sniggered into his hand. But Jigsaw was delighted, and laughed with glee.

'Thank you, father, thank you indeed,' he said. 'It is the quaintest, smoothest walking-stick that ever I saw.'

'The poor silly,' said Noughts-and-Crosses.

'How he simpers,' said Snakes-and-Ladders.

And they bowed to their father, and went off down the three hundred stairs, tip, tap, tip, tap, tippety-tap. Jigsaw stayed behind to make his father comfortable. He puffed up his pillows and laid a log on the fire.

'If you call to it twice, it will come to your aid,' said the old baron sleepily, muttering into his beard. And in a flicker of a flame he was fast asleep.

'I suppose he means the stick,' said Jigsaw to himself. And he did a hop, skip and jump towards the door, for he loved his walking-stick.

Now Noughts-and-Crosses, the eldest son, was too cross to get on well with the cows. When he tried to drive them they went the wrong direction, and when he tried to milk them, they kicked over the pail. So whenever he could, he made Jigsaw do his work.

'Hi, come here, Lazybones, and drive the cows up out of this field,' said he crossly one day to his brother. The field was very large and the cows were very many and far away, and Jigsaw had no dog. 'But,' thought he, 'I have my walking-stick.' So he said, very quietly:

'Stick, stick, wake up quick.'

And in no time, in the twinkle of a cow-heel, there was the stick running over the field on a pair of spindly legs, and wavings its spindly arms at the cows! You would have laughed to see it, as Jigsaw did. It tapped them, and flicked them and drove them all along.

'Mercy me!' said Noughts-and-Crosses watching, 'the stick's bewitched, bewitched it is! I tell you what, Jigsaw, I'll give you a bag of gold for that stick.'

'I wouldn't part with my stick for a hundred bags of gold,' said Jigsaw, merrily. And off he went to the courtyard.

In the courtyard was Snakes-and-Ladders, selling fruit and vegetables to the villagers. Jigsaw stood behind the stall to watch. Every time Snakes-and-Ladders weighed a pound of apples he put in a bad one. The village folk muttered, and the bravest grumbled, but Snakes-and-Ladders only smiled slyly and said: 'Take it or leave it, take it or leave it!'

'This is not fair,' said Jigsaw softly. 'Stick, stick, help me quick,' said he, in a whisper. And, quick as you like, away jumped the stick and set upon

Snakes-and-Ladders. It beat him round the court-yard, it beat him under the stall, it beat him and beat him, up the steps and down again! How the people laughed! They laughed till they cried, the old ones and the young ones.

'Stop, stop, stop,' cried Snakes-and-Ladders all the time. 'Stop the stick, someone, and I'll give you all good apples!'

At this the stick stopped and went back to its master. Snakes-and-Ladders grumbled, but he changed all the apples. And he said to his brother, 'Listen here, Jigsaw. I'll give you a bag of silver if you'll sell the walking-stick.'

'That I won't, for a thousand bags of silver,' said Jigsaw merrily, and he went off whistling.

That night, as he lay on his bed, the walking-stick stood up from its place in the corner and came over to Jigsaw, as jaunty as a robin. 'Master,' whispered the stick, 'your brothers want to steal me. I think I'd better run away and hide in the wood.' And it smiled and winked with its ivory eyes.

'Then off you go,' said Jigsaw laughing, 'and wait till I come for you.'

Off went the stick, snip, snap, out of the window,

down the wall, across the moat, and out of sight into the woods.

Jigsaw slept with one ear open, and in the middle of the night he heard creak, creak and shuffle and sniff. In came his brothers in their nightcaps to steal the walking-stick. They hunted and hunted and then they grew angry.

'Wake up, Jigsaw! Where's the walking-stick?'

'It ran away and left me,' said Jigsaw, sobbing. 'What shall I do without it, I'd like to know!' And he sniffed and snivelled and pretended to be sad.

'Then you can just go after it,' said Noughts-and-Crosses, gruffly. 'And you needn't come back without the walking-stick.'

'But where shall I go if I can't find the stick?'

'You'd better go to the palace and marry the princess,' said Snakes-and-Ladders. And he laughed till he cried, he thought this such a joke.

They let down the drawbridge and off went Jigsaw as merry as a lark. When he reached the wood, his walking-stick was waiting.

'We won't go back there,' it said, 'that we will *not*.'

'Then where shall we go?' said Jigsaw.

'We'll go to the palace, and marry the princess.'

'Bless my soul,' said Jigsaw, 'you are a merry fellow. I don't care where I go as long as you come with me.'

That night they made a fire and slept in the forest: but the next day they walked until they reached the palace. Now the King and Queen of Tiddleywinks had lately died, and their aunt ruled the kingdom because the princess was too young. Poor Princess Dominoes! What a time she had with her great-aunt Crossword! She made her count goose feathers, she made her spin nettles, she made her carry water and do the washing-up. When Jigsaw arrived she was sweeping out the courtyard.

'Good-morning,' said he. 'Is the princess to be seen?'

'I'm the princess, though I know you wouldn't think it,' and she dropped him a curtsey, and wiped away a tear.

'I can't stand and see a princess sweeping out the courtyard,' said Jigsaw gallantly. And he took the broom and swept for her, while she told him all about her great-aunt Crossword, and he told

94

her all about the baron, his father, and the three hundred stairs.

Now the cross old great-aunt was watching from a window, to see that the princess did her work.

'Crimp my curls!' exclaimed she crossly. 'Who's the girl talking to now?' And she ran down the steps and across the yard.

'I'll teach you to waste time talking to visitors! I'll shut you up with bread and water for a week!' she screamed, and started to chase the princess.

'Stick, stick, trip her up quick!' said Jigsaw. And away flew the stick and hopped in front of the cross old great-aunt and down fell she, flat, while the stick beat her and beat her and danced all round in a frenzy.

'Mercy on us, the thing's enchanted! Call it off! Help, help!' gasped great-aunt Crossword.

At this Jigsaw came up as bold as a brass farthing and said,

'What will you give me if I call off the stick?'

'Anything you mention from a pumpkin to a pomegranate,' said she, screaming.

'I don't want a pumpkin and I don't want a pomegranate, but I *do* want the Princess Dominoes,' said Jigsaw.

95

'All right, all right,' shouted the old great-aunt. 'You shall have the princess and much good may she do you.'

So the stick stopped beating and the great-aunt scrambled up and they all went inside to draw up the marriage settlement.

Now on the day that Jigsaw was married to the Princess Dominoes, the stick came sidling up to its master and mistress, with its ivory face rather sad.

'Master,' said the stick, 'I have made you happy, and the spell is over. From this day on I am a plain, ordinary stick.' And that was the last time the walking-stick spoke.

But Jigsaw and the Princess Dominoes loved it dearly, and she polished it every day and never forgot it. And when her children were bad or sad, or grumpy, she could always make them laugh with the story of the stick.

The House with Two Doors

THERE was once a large family of rabbits who lived in a rambling house under a little hill. They had two main doors to their house, one at the front of the hill facing the meadow where the mushrooms grew, and one at the side of the hill opposite a ploughed field. This was the back door, and was marked by an old rotten stump. The front door was grander, having several holes into it, and marked by a thorn bush – 'For,' said James Rabbit, 'if ever I happen to be the other side of my house, and I want to get in in rather a hurry, I must have a door to get in at.'

Mrs Jane Rabbit agreed with this heartily, and she used to say to her children:

'Now if ever you are in the meadow and want to get home in a hurry, remember to look for the thorn tree. And if ever you are in the field, and need to come in quickly, remember to look for the old rotten stump.' So the children did.

One evening in winter-time James Rabbit, who was feeling very hungry, said he was going out to look for something to eat. He said that he did not know whether he would find anything, because this was the wrong time of year for really good things to eat, such as lettuce and turnip tops. But he would go out and try. At this the children, who were playing at one end of the kitchen, bobbed up, very excited, and said that they would come too.

'Please let us come, too,' they cried. Jane Rabbit looked doubtful.

'I think that it is too cold for a family of rabbits to go out,' said she.

'On the other hand,' said she, 'if you go out with your father and he finds you something to eat, then I shan't have to.'

James Rabbit went to the door, put his nose out a very little way and wriggled it. It was a cold

night. Then he pattered back along the passage.

'My dear,' he said to his wife, 'I don't think it will hurt the children if they run about to keep warm. We shall not be gone for long.' And he took off his bedroom-slippers and put on his boots.

'All right,' said Jane Rabbit, 'but they must wear coats and mufflers.'

'Hurrah, hurrah!' said the young rabbits, and the youngest tried to escape without his scarf. Mrs Rabbit caught him by the hind leg.

'I shall stay at home,' said she, 'and have hot soup ready for when you come in.'

So off they went. Mrs Rabbit went to the front door and saw them off into the field.

'Now, if you want to get in in a hurry, remember the stump and the thorn bush,' she called.

But the family were half-way across the meadow. James Rabbit led the way through the ditch into a field where the farmer grew sugar beet. As it was December, most of the sugar beet had been taken up and put into large piles, waiting for lorries to come and collect them. But a few odd ones lay here and there.

'Good food for rabbits,' said James, 'now, run off, but do not go out of sight. If I call, then come at once.'

So a rabbit called Winkle chased off at once over the clods of earth to where he saw a large white beet glimmering. The rest scattered, and were soon hard at work eating their supper. The youngest, Puff, was a timid, shy rabbit and preferred to stay near the hedge eating some tops which had been cut off the beet.

As for James, he made for a great pile of straw, and nibbled and nibbled and scratched until he uncovered a beautiful yellow vegetable at the bottom. And this he began to eat. A little farther along the pile there was a rat, eating another of the juicy vegetables. But James didn't speak to him, and he didn't speak to James. There was plenty for both.

Well, it grew colder and colder that night, and Winkle and his brothers ran farther and farther to keep warm. The wind began to blow, and the snow began to snow, and Winkle looked around him and could see nothing for the whirling white flakes. It snowed and snowed very hard for a long time. But instead of going home, Winkle and his brothers, who had not seen snow before, stayed out in the field, and chased each other and rolled each other and threw snow-balls, and wandered farther and farther. All except Puff, and when he felt the great soft flakes coming down on *his* head, he darted under the hedge near somebody's door, and took shelter. And every time he peeped out to see how the meadow was getting on, he grew a white lace cap on his head which was pretty, but cold.

'Well,' thought Puff, after quite a long while, 'if I don't go home soon, I shan't get home tonight. The meadow is all white instead of dark.'

So he set off towards the thorn bush. But when he got there, he could see the thorn bush, but he could not see the front door at all. 'Perhaps this is the wrong thorn bush,' thought Puff. But he remembered the shape of the branches. 'The fact is,' he said, 'this white stuff has covered up the door. I had better go round to the rotten stump.'

When he got there he met most of his brothers, who had walked round in a ring and come home again.

'It's a very funny thing,' said Puff, 'but there is no door at the thorn tree at all.'

'That is a nuisance,' said Winkle, 'for there's no door at this stump either.'

'Perhaps we have come to the wrong hill,' said one.

'Nonsense,' said Puff, who was clever though shy, 'it is this white stuff which has covered everything up.'

'Well, how are we to get in? I am cold,' said another.

'We must dig,' said Puff.

'Let's go to the thorn bush, then, for that door is better,' said Winkle, 'and nearer home.'

When they got to the front door, or what used to be the front door, whom should they meet but James, looking very white. For he had gone on at his very tasty vegetable a long time before he grew too cold to eat any more.

'Here's a pleasant to-do,' said James to his children. 'We are snowed-out.'

'Snowed-out?' said Puff.

'This stuff is snow,' said James. 'It is quite soft, and we must dig. Mrs Rabbit will be in a great stew thinking we are lost.'

So they copied their

father as he scratched and scraped and scrabbled. All in a row they stood, trying to get in at their front door. (I saw their footmarks the next morning.)

Meanwhile Mrs Rabbit was very worried. 'Where can they be?' she said. 'I shall go to the door and see.' When she got there, there wasn't a door, but a wall of white snow. 'Who has done this?' said Mrs Rabbit, crossly. 'This is not funny at all. I shall go to the other door.' But it was just the same that end. So Mrs Rabbit fetched her broom and began sweeping.

'Tut, tut!' she muttered, 'such a mess and such floods as we shall have!'

There seemed to be a lot of snow. By and by, she thought she heard voices. Soon she knew she could hear voices.

'Come on,' said James's voice, 'we're nearly there!'

'Nearly there! Nearly there!' said Winkle's voice.

And then they all tumbled in on top of Mrs Rabbit and her broom.

'Dear, dear, *what* a mess,' said Mrs Rabbit. 'But come into the warm and have some good soup.'

'We were snowed-out, snowed-out,' said Puff, excitedly.

'Both ends,' said Winkle.

'Very deep drifts,' said James, wisely.

'Yes, don't I know,' said Mrs Jane Rabbit.

How the Donkey Found a Master

THERE was once a donkey whose name was
Daisy, and she had a fluffy baby called Dick who
lived with her in a thistle field. His ears were very
large, and very silky, and his nose was as soft as
velvet, and when his mother wanted him, she
said: 'Eeyore! Eeyore!'

They both belonged to an old man called Mr
Pretty who grew vegetables. When he had grown

enough to sell, he put them on a little cart, and Daisy pulled the cart all round the nearby villages, for the people to buy Mr Pretty's beautiful vegetables. But what about Dick? The first time his mother left him to go round with the cart he was very lonely. He came to the gate of the thistle field and saw her out.

'Now, I shan't be long,' said his mother, rubbing his nose. And Mr Pretty patted him and told him to be a good donkey. So he stood and watched until he could not see the red radishes and crispy lettuces on the cart any more, and then he went back into his field and ate a thistle.

'Crunch, crunch, crunch, crunch,' said Dick. 'These are pretty good prickly thistles.'

Now when the donkey was a little older Mr Pretty came down to the field and looked sadly at Daisy, and then at Dick.

And he said:

'I'm afraid I shall have to sell 'ee, little donkey.'

Daisy said: 'Eeyore! Eeyore!' For she felt sad.

'I will not be sold to somebody I do not like,' said the donkey to his mother. 'I shall go and find my own master.'

'Dearie me!' sighed his mother, 'I wish you

needn't be sold at all. Do you think you can find a master in this village?'

'Yes,' said Dick, 'that is just what I shall do.'

So one day when the gate was left open by mistake, he went out into the street and trotted along towards the village. 'Tittle-tup, tittle-tup, tittle-tup, tittle-tup' twinkled his neat little feet.

The donkey was very pleased, because this was the first time he had been out of his field. Soon he came to a hole in the hedge, and he went in to the farmer's field and sniffed the ground. Young, juicy, crisp carrots! He pulled one up and ate it. Crunch, crunchety, crunch. And he pulled another up and ate it. It tasted lovely. But when he had eaten nine or ten, some men working in the field saw him.

'Hi! There's old Pretty's donkey eating farmer's carrots! Shoo!' And they ran towards him. The donkey did not wait to hear what *they* had to say, but turned and trotted on down the street.

'Tittle-tup, tittle-tup, tittle-tup, tittle-tup,' went his neat little feet.

'*They* wouldn't do for masters,' said he.

And he came to the village pond. He was thirsty with all his trotting, so he went down to the water

to have a drink. There he met a horse, having a drink as well. The horse shook the flies off with his mane and said:

'Who do *you* belong to?'

'Mr Pretty,' said the donkey, 'but I am out looking for a new master.'

And just then the horse's master, who was standing by his cart, said:

'Hey! Isn't that old Pretty's donkey got out of his field? I'll catch him.' And he started to run. But the donkey ran faster, round the pond and down the street.

'Ti-*tup*, ti-*tup*, ti-*tup*, ti-*tup*,' went his little feet, cantering.

'I don't want *him* for a master,' he said.

Soon he came to the end of the village, where there was a little cottage all by itself, in which the shoe-mender lived. Leaning over the shoe-mender's gate was the shoe-mender's little boy, Peter.

'Hullo!' said Peter. 'A whiffly grey donkey! I wish I could have him!'

When the donkey heard this, he stopped and came up to the gate, and pushed his velvet nose at Peter's coat.

'I like you,' said Peter. 'I wish you'd come into my garden.'

So he opened the gate and the donkey came in and stood flicking his ears, with his feet together.

'Dad,' called Peter, 'look who's come to see me!'

'Why,' said his father, coming out, 'that's old Pretty's donkey. We shall have to take him back. He's run away.'

'But I want him. I could ride him beautifully,' said Peter.

His father went into his workshop, and he

fetched a little red saddle and a harness, and put them on. And the donkey stood as good as gold.

'Well,' said his father, 'he's a very well behaved donkey. Get on, and we'll go back and see Mr. Pretty.'

So they did. T-i-t-t-l-e – tup, t-i-t-t-l-e – tup, t-i-t-t-l-e – tup, went the donkey's feet, walking slowly. When they got to the thistle field, there was Daisy. She said: 'Eeyore! Eeyore!' For she thought Dick was lost. Mr Pretty came hibbledy, hobbledy, up to the gate.

'Do you want to sell this very nice donkey of yours?' said the shoe-mender to Mr Pretty.

'That's just what I shall have to do,' said Mr Pretty.

'If I bought him for my little boy, could he live in this field and share that shed? For I haven't a field of my own.'

'Yes, he could,' said Mr Pretty. 'If you will look after him and buy his oats.'

So they settled it between them. And Peter was very pleased, and used to ride Dick every day. Sometimes they met Mr Pretty with his cart, and then Dick and Daisy stopped to talk to each other and rub noses.

'Eeyore!' said Daisy. 'I shall see you tonight.'

And each evening they both came back to their thistle field. Dick was proud of his new red saddle, and Peter was very proud of Dick. And Daisy was as happy as could be.

The Picnic

JANE, Susan and Julia went for a picnic with their mother and father. It was a beautiful, hot sunny day in August, so they went down to be near the sea in a quiet place where there were not many other people. They left the car on a grassy path, and below the path were some flat hot stones and below the stones some white sand and below the sand the sea.

Susan and Julia took off their sandals and ran down to the sea to paddle, but Jane, who was older, wanted to help her father.

'First we put seven big stones in a ring on the

sand to make a fireplace,' said father. 'You get some too. One – two – three – four – five – six – seven. Good.'

'What do we do next?' said Jane.

'Next, we fetch little bits of dry wood and dry grass,' said father, 'to make the fire, to cook our dinner,' he said.

Jane went running along looking for pieces of dry wood, over the sand, over the stones, up to the grassy path.

All of a sudden, Jane called:

'Daddy! Daddy! Look what I've found! Come quickly! Come and see!'

Daddy ran after Jane to see what she had found, and mummy ran after daddy and Susan and Julia ran after mummy to see what Jane had found.

Can you guess?

They couldn't.

In the grassy path there were some stony places; and in one of the stony places there was a little hole, and in the doorway of the hole there sat –

'A little darling, brown MOUSE!' said Jane.

'Let me see, let me see!' said Susan and Julia.

'Be careful, you may frighten him away,' said mother.

But the mouse was not at all frightened. He sat up and cleaned his big whiskers as Jane had seen a cat do.

'Oh! Isn't he a sweet mouse!' she said. 'He's mine. I found him. I shall call him Ransome. Do you think I could stroke him?'

'You could try, very gently, with one finger,' said father.

Jane did. The mouse was not afraid. He came out of his hole and sat in the sun. And after him came –

'Another MOUSE!' said Susan. 'That's my mouse, I saw him come, I shall call him . . . I shall call him Nutty.' And Susan stroked her mouse.

'I want a mouse. I want to stroke them,' said Julia.

Mother picked up Ransome, very gently, and put him in Julia's hand. She giggled and shivered because he tickled. She put him down quickly.

Ransome and Nutty played with each other in the sun. They ran, and sat up, and stroked their whiskers, they lay in the sun and blinked their eyes. They lolled against each other. The children watched them for a long time.

'They must have a nest in there,' said mother.

'Well, come on,' said father, 'the fire is burning brightly, and it is time to cook our dinner.'

Mother put the sausages in the frying pan and pricked them all, prick, prick, prick, with a fork. Soon they were sizzling in the pan over the fire father had made. Can you imagine them, fat and brown?

'The mice want their dinner,' Jane said.

'You shall give the mice some dinner when you've had yours,' said mother.

So when they had eaten the sausages, Jane, Susan and Julia took some crumbs to the mice. Ransome and Nutty twitched their noses.

'Crumbs,' said Jane.

The mice sat up on their hind legs, picked the

crumbs up in their little neat paws, and began to eat them.

'They're eating them!' said Jane.

'They love them!' said Susan.

'They want some more!' said Julia.

Mother cut up a piece of cheese into tiny, tiny pieces.

The mice loved the cheese, too, although they were field-mice, not house-mice who sometimes steal cheese.

'Let's make a little garden to their house,' said Jane.

Jane, Susan and Julia found some small grey stones and they made a little wall all round the hole where Ransome and Nutty lived. They put some grass in the garden. The mice ran round their garden, hopping at each other and playing games.

'What a good thing there isn't a cat or a dog near,' said Jane.

Sometimes the mice jumped over their wall, and went to see the world. When they were tired and full of cheese, they went to sleep. If they got too hot, they lay in the shade of one of the stones.

'Perhaps they would like a drink,' Susan said.

Father gave the mice a drink in the lid of his tobacco tin. Susan put it in the mouse garden. First Nutty, and then Ransome, came to sniff and have a drink of cool water.

'Aren't they clever mice?' said Jane.

'I want one of my own,' said Julia.

'You can share Ransome,' said Jane.

'And Nutty,' said Susan.

'No, I want a mouse of my own,' said Julia.

All day long, between paddling, the children played with the friendly field-mice.

After tea father played ball with Jane and Susan, while Julia went to see the mice. She lay on her tummy, on the grassy path, and stroked Ransome. He was so soft, so small, so neat and so nice, she did want one of her own.

All of a sudden there came walking along the path rather slowly. . . . Can you guess?

'Another MOUSE!' said Julia softly, so as not to frighten her.

'Do you live here?' said Julia to the mouse.

When the third mouse came

to the hole she sniffed, and she twinkled her eyes at Julia, and she looked surprised at the little grey wall. Then over she went, hop, skip and long tail into the mouse garden, to play with Ransome and Nutty.

'She DOES live here!' said Julia.

'Mummy! Daddy! I've got a mouse! My mouse has come home, another mouse!'

Daddy ran to see Julia's mouse, and mummy ran after daddy, and Jane after mummy and Susan and Julia last of all.

'Well, isn't that a good thing,' said daddy.

'I expect he had been out for the day,' said mummy. 'What is *his* name?'

'Julia,' said Julia, stroking her mouse.

'And a very nice name, too. I expect she's their sister.'

'Yes,' said Julia.

'If only we could take them home,' said Jane.

'Yes!' said Susan. 'If only we could!'

'They will be so much happier in their own little house,' said mother. 'And you have had them for a whole long day to play with. Besides, the cat next door might catch them.'

'Nearly time to go home,' said father.

'But supposing someone comes along this path and treads on them?' said Jane.

'We will put up a notice,' father said.

So he found a flat stone and mother found a piece of chalk and they wrote on it:

BE CAREFUL : MICE PLAYING

And they put it near the mouse garden. Then Jane, Susan and Julia said goodbye to Ransome, Nutty and their sister Julia, and climbed into the car and went home to bed.

And when it grew dark and cool, Ransome, Nutty and their sister Julia went into their nest in their hole, and went to bed too.

Jane thought of them before she went to sleep, as snug and warm as she was.

ABOUT THE AUTHOR

Helen Clare's real name is Pauline Clarke. She was born in Nottingham, and gained an M.A. degree from Oxford University. She is married to a history don, and lives in Cambridge.

Under her own name Miss Clarke has had eighteen books for children published, of which the best known is *The Twelve and the Genii*, which won the Carnegie Medal in 1962.

Under the pseudonym of Helen Clare she has written *Merlin's Magic*, *Seven White Pebbles*, and five books in the series beginning with *Five Dolls in a House* (which is also available as a Young Puffin).

SOME OTHER YOUNG PUFFINS

FIVE DOLLS IN A HOUSE *Helen Clare*

A little girl called Elizabeth finds a way of making herself small and visits her dolls in their own house.

THE URCHIN *Edith Unnerstad*

The Urchin is only five years old – but already he has the Larsson family at sixes and sevens with his ingenious tricks and adventures.

SOMETHING TO DO *Septima*

This is a book full of suggestions for games to play and things to make and do each month, from January to December. It is designed to help mothers with young children at home. (*Original*)

A BROTHER FOR THE OPHELINES *Natalie Savage Carlson*

Sequel to *The Happy Orpheline*. Josine, smallest of all the orphans, finds a baby left on the doorstep. But it is a *boy*. So the orphans plot and worry to find a way to keep him.

MAGIC IN MY POCKET *Alison Uttley*

A selection of short stories by this well-loved author, especially good for five and six years olds.

THE SECRET SHOEMAKERS *James Reeves*

James Reeves has searched through the whole range of stories the Brothers Grimm collected, chosen a dozen of the best, least well-known stories, and told them with all a poet's magic. Illustrated by Edward Ardizzone.

FLAT STANLEY *Jeff Brown and Tomi Ungerer*

Stanley Lambchop was an ordinary boy, except for one thing: he was four feet tall, about a foot wide, and only half an inch thick! This is one of the funniest and most original books for young children to appear for years.

TALES FROM THE END COTTAGE *Eileen Bell*

George and Shoosh were tabby cats and they lived with Tooty, a very pretty Peke, in Mrs Apple's cottage in Northamptonshire. They led a pleasant quiet life, until Black Dog came knocking on the door seeking refuge from the gypsies. (*Original*)

THE YOUNG PUFFIN BOOK OF VERSE ed. *Barbara Ireson*

A deluge of poems about such fascinating subjects as birds and balloons, mice and moonshine, farmers and frogs, pigeons and pirates, especially chosen to please young people of four to eight.

THE CASTLE OF YEW *Lucy M. Boston*

Joseph visits the magic garden where the yew trees are shaped like castles and finds himself shrunk small enough to crawl inside one.

LITTLE OLD MRS PEPPERPOT
MRS PEPPERPOT TO THE RESCUE *Alf Prøysen*

Gay little stories about an old woman who suddenly shrinks to the size of a pepperpot.

PONDER AND WILLIAM
PONDER AND WILLIAM ON HOLIDAY *Barbara Softly*

Ponder the panda looks after William's pyjamas and is a wonderful companion in these all the year round adventures. Illustrated by Diana John. (*Originals*)